Uncle Dick
(gone to
warmer climes)

Aunt Violet

Aunt Hatty

both eaten by ginger cat

Uncle Terry - Aunt June
(charlie's parents)

Tim Zizi Bob Jojo Blodwyn Cy Pearl Gus Danny Lily Iris Micky Peregrine

(Cousins)

VIKING KESTREL
Viking Penguin Inc., 40 West 23rd Street, New York, New York 10010, U.S.A.

Copyright © Wendy Smith, 1986
All rights reserved
Published in Great Britain by J. M. Dent & Sons Ltd 1986
First published in the United States of America by Viking Penguin Inc. 1986
Printed in Denmark
1 2 3 4 5 90 89 88 87 86

Library of Congress catalog card number: 86-40013
(CIP data available)
ISBN 0-670-81251-X

Wendy Smith
The Lonely, Only Mouse

Viking Kestrel

Thelonius had no brothers or sisters.
"Isn't that rather strange for a mouse?" he wondered.

"Why am I an only mouse?" he asked his mother.
"Just because," she replied. "Now do leave me to get on with
my woodwork."

Thelonius went to his bedroom and sulked.
"It would be such fun to have a brother to play with," he said
to himself.

Just then his mother popped her nose around the door.

"Hurry up, Thelonius, and set the table. Father will be home any minute!"

Thelonius made a special effort to make the table look nice.

"Maybe Father will play soccer after dinner if he's pleased with me," he thought.

Father brought home a lovely, squishy, smelly lump of Gorgonzola.

They all ate so much that after dinner they could hardly move.

"Off to bed now, young Thelonius.
We'll play soccer another day," said Father.
"Your mother and I want some peace."

But Thelonius was so full that his stomach ached and he could
not sleep.
"If I had a sister," he thought, "she would stroke my whiskers
and make me feel better."

The next day it poured, so Thelonius had to stay inside.

"Will you play tiddlywinks, Mother?" he asked.
"Not now, darling, I'm too busy. Ask your Father."

But Father was about to go to the Laundromat.
"You'll have to learn to amuse yourself, my boy," he said.

Thelonius tried playing tiddlywinks on his own, but it was boring. "An only mouse is a lonely mouse," he said, sighing.

Then he had an idea.

"I'll go and find myself a brother," he decided, and scampered off to see the dog.

"Will you be my brother?" he asked.

"I'm too busy being man's best friend," the dog replied. "Why not try the parakeet?"

"Will you be my brother?" he asked.
"Who's a pretty boy?" chirped the parakeet.
"What did you say?" asked Thelonius.
"Joey's a pretty boy," the bird answered.

Thelonius gave up and went to ask the goldfish.

"Will you be my brother and sister?"

"Pwop, pwop" was all they had to say.

Finally, he went to ask the pig down the road
if she'd be his sister, but she smelled so
funny he thought better of it.

Since Thelonius couldn't think of anyone else to ask,
he went home.

When he arrived he found his mother had a surprise for him.

"You remember your cousin Charlie?" she said.
"He's going to spend the night with us. You will take care of him,
won't you?"

"Like a brother!" replied Thelonius.

It was still raining, so they watched television.

"What should we look at? You choose, Charlie," said Thelonius.
"There's a soccer match on soon," he suggested helpfully.

But they didn't watch Thelonius's favorite sports program.

Instead, they watched a nature film on slugs.

At supper, Thelonius offered Charlie the cheeseboard.
"Guests first," he said politely.
Charlie took all the soft cheese with the herby bits. Thelonius
had the old, hard lump left over from the week before.

When it was time to bathe, Charlie used all the hot water.

"Enjoy yourself!" said Thelonius, scrubbing Charlie's back.
Charlie had a great time, splashing water everywhere,
and leaving Thelonius to mop up the puddles.

The water was barely lukewarm for Thelonius,
and, what's more, Charlie had used all the bubble bath.

Needless to say, Thelonius gave Charlie his bed.
He was peacefully reading his favorite story on the sofa before
turning out the light when Charlie appeared.

"Your mattress is too soft," he complained.
"And I'm lonely without my twenty-five brothers and sisters!"

So Charlie, too, slept on the sofa. His feet were hard and cold.
Worse still, he snored.

"Is this what they call brotherly love?" Thelonius wondered.

The following morning, while Charlie lingered over a second helping of cereal, Thelonius went to pack Charlie's bag.

"Speed the parting guest," he said, yawning .

He was surprised to see how few things Charlie had — just a scruffy old toothbrush, a bald teddy, and a fossilized cheese sandwich. Even the bag had seen better days.

Thelonius looked at his own toothbrush . . .   and at his bears.

He bounced on his comfortable bed.

He thought of hot baths,

huge, smelly cheeses,

good books,

and soccer with Father.

He thought about never having to watch a nature film on slugs, and about Charlie . . .

. . . and Charlie's brothers and sisters.

"I like being an only mouse," Thelonius decided.
"An only mouse has his moments."

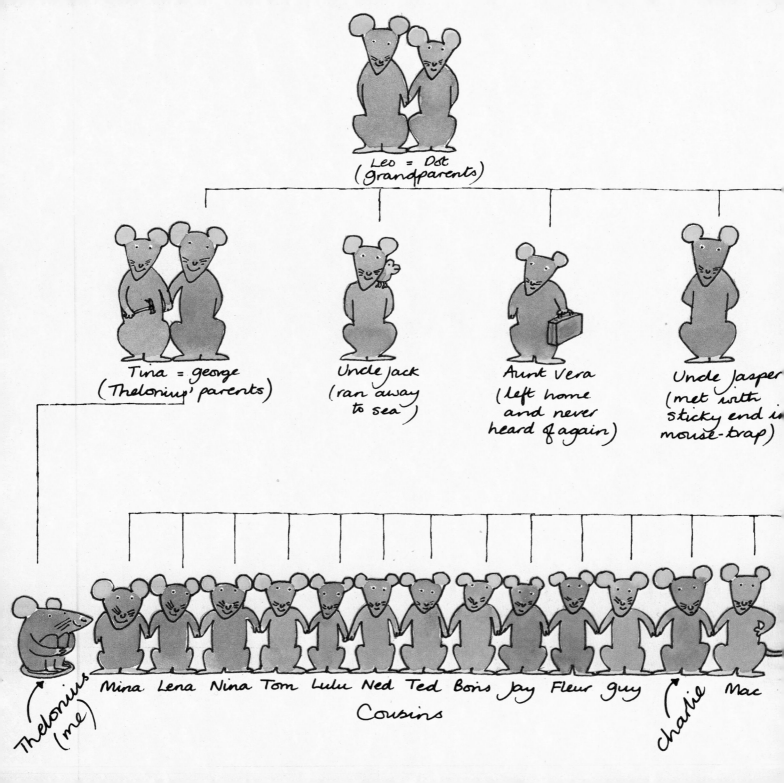

Leo = Dot
(grandparents)

Tina = george
(Thelonius' parents)

Uncle Jack
(ran away
to sea)

Aunt Vera
(left home
and never
heard of again)

Uncle Jasper
(met with
sticky end i
mouse-trap)

Thelonius
(me)

Mina Lena Nina Tom Lulu Ned Ted Boris Jay Fleur guy Charlie Mac
Cousins